# I AM BRAVE ONLINE

RACHAEL MORLOCK

**PowerKiDS** press

NEW YORK

Published in 2020 by The Rosen Publishing Group, Inc.
29 East 21st Street, New York, NY 10010

First Edition

Editor: Elizabeth Krajnik
Book Design: Reann Nye

Photo Credits: Cover Syda Productions/Shutterstock.com; p. 5 Rawpixel.com/Shutterstock.com; p. 7 Tyler Olson/Shutterstock.com; pp. 9, 21 Monkey Business Images/Shutterstock.com; p. 11 bbernard/Shutterstock.com; p. 13 Jasmin Merdan/Moment/Getty Images; p. 15 wavebreakmedia/Shutterstock.com; p. 17 Daisy Daisy/Shutterstock.com; p. 19 Hero Images/Getty Images; p. 22 vectorfusionart/Shutterstock.com.

Cataloging-in-Publication Data

Names: Morlock, Rachael.
Title: I am brave online / Rachael Morlock.
Description: New York : PowerKids Press, 2020. | Series: I am a good digital citizen | Includes glossary and index.
Identifiers: ISBN 9781538349526 (pbk.) | ISBN 9781538349540 (library bound) | ISBN 9781538349533 (6pack)
Subjects: LCSH: Cyberbullying–Juvenile literature. | Internet and children–Juvenile literature.
Classification: LCC HV6773.15.C92 M67 2020 | DDC 302.34'302854678–dc23

Manufactured in the United States of America

CPSIA Compliance Information: Batch #CSPK19. For Further Information contact Rosen Publishing, New York, New York at 1-800-237-9932.

# CONTENTS

# BRAVE CITIZENS

If you use the Internet, then you're a digital citizen. Good digital citizens follow rules for safety, kindness, and fairness online. Their actions make the Internet better for everyone. But it isn't always easy to do the right thing. Good digital citizens have to be brave.

# CALLING ON COURAGE

The Internet is large, busy, and sometimes frightening. It takes **courage** to **explore** the online world. It can take even more courage to talk about what you find. Tell others when you or someone else is in trouble. It's one of the bravest things you can do as a digital citizen.

# SPEAK UP!

Have you ever felt sad, scared, or worried about something you saw online? Maybe you saw an **upsetting** picture, read an unkind **comment**, or heard something you know is untrue. You can't control everything you see online, but you can control what you do. It's hard but important to speak up when something's wrong.

9

# TALK IT OUT

Talking about a problem can help you deal with it. Try talking with a parent or another trusted adult. Tell them how you feel and why. Their ideas can help you decide what to do next. You might also come up with new rules to help you stay safe online.

# ASK FOR HELP

It's not your fault when something scary happens online. You can have a problem even when you're careful and follow the rules. Some problems can be fixed at home, but you may need extra help to fix others. You can get help from teachers, principals, **counselors**, and police officers.

13

# CYBERBULLYING

Cyberbullying is when people use **technology** and the Internet to send others hurtful messages. It's a common problem for young digital citizens. Cyberbullying might happen only once or it might happen regularly over time. Bullying is powerful, **harmful**, and very **serious**. When you see cyberbullying, you need to say something.

# SPOTTING CYBERBULLYING

Cyberbullying can happen through text messages, emails, and **social media**. Cyberbullies may use a hurtful message, a mean story, an unwanted nickname, or an **embarrassing** picture to bully someone. Cyberbullying can come from one person or a group of people. You can spot it in any messages that are meant to make someone feel bad.

# BEING BULLIED

If you've been cyberbullied, you might not want to talk about it. Maybe you're worried that you won't be allowed on the Internet anymore. You must be brave in order to speak up. Don't talk back to the bully. Instead, tell an adult what's happening and report it to the app or website it happened on.

19

# HELPING OTHERS

You can report cyberbullying even when it's not happening to you. If you know someone is being bullied, try showing them extra kindness online or in person. Let them know you care! Set a good example with the things you share online. With courage, you can stand up against cyberbullying.

# BRAVER TOGETHER

Talking to trusted adults about what you do online is an important part of being a good digital citizen. You can tell an adult about online problems, but it's also fun to share good things. Show your parents and teachers how you use the Internet. Try bravely exploring and learning together!

# GLOSSARY

**comment:** An expression of opinion either in speech or writing.

**counselor:** A person who gives advice.

**courage:** The ability to do something dangerous or difficult.

**embarrassing:** Causing someone to feel foolish in front of others.

**explore:** To search something to find out more about it.

**harmful:** Causing or capable of causing damage or harm.

**serious:** Deserving much care or attention.

**social media:** Forms of online communication through which people create online communities to share knowledge, ideas, personal messages, etc.

**technology:** The way people do something and the tools they use.

**upsetting:** Causing someone to worry or be unhappy.

# INDEX

# WEBSITES

Due to the changing nature of Internet links, PowerKids Press has developed an online list of websites related to the subject of this book. This site is updated regularly. Please use this link to access the list: www.powerkidslinks.com/digcit/brave